?

IF LOOKS COULD KILL

"Gorgons don't just vanish into thin air," Warren said.

"There's nowhere else for her to hide." Rick paused. "Unless she's behind the—"

His eyes opened wide. A horrid shriek erupted from behind the stairs and clammy, leathery wings exploded into Warren's face. He slammed his eyes shut and beat the Gorgon off, hearing Rick's sword swish through empty air. Warren dove back, rolled on his shoulder, and came up clear, his sword slicing in every direction and his eyes fixed on his shield as he flashed it around the basement.

The Gorgon was perched on Harper's stony arm. She was sixty pounds of boiled-down ugly with a face like a living nightmare. Snakes danced around her head, hissing and striking at Rick's sword as he waved it in the air. Her gold-and-black eyes were slit like a cat's, and her teeth were in worse shape than Princey's.

With one clawed hand, she gathered the dust off the top of a pipe and threw it at Rick's shield.

"Aagh! She messed up my shield! I can't see a thing!"

Panic crawled across Rick's face, the same look that was frozen on Harper's. He dropped his shield and turned toward the Gorgon.

"Don't look, Rick!"

YEARLING BOOKS are designed especially to entertain and enlighten young people. Patricia Reilly Giff, consultant to this series, received her bachelor's degree from Marymount College and a master's degree in history from St. John's University. She holds a Professional Diploma in Reading and a Doctorate of Humane Letters from Hofstra University. She was a teacher and reading consultant for many years, and is the author of numerous books for young readers.

For a complete listing of all Yearling titles,
write to
Dell Readers Service,
P.O. Box 1045,
South Holland, IL 60473.

GARY PAULSEN
WORLD OF ADVENTURE

THE
GORGON
SLAYER

A YEARLING BOOK

Published by
Bantam Doubleday Dell Books for Young Readers
a division of
Bantam Doubleday Dell Publishing Group, Inc.
1540 Broadway
New York, New York 10036

ISBN: 0-440-41041-X

Series design: Barbara Berger

Interior illustration by Michael David Biegel

Printed in the United States of America

October 1995

OPM   10   9   8   7   6   5   4   3   2   1

Dear Readers:

Real adventure is many things—it's danger and daring and sometimes even a struggle for life or death. From competing in the Iditarod dogsled race across Alaska to sailing the Pacific Ocean, I've experienced some of this adventure myself. I try to capture this spirit in my stories, and each time I sit down to write, that challenge is a bit of an adventure in itself.

You're all a part of this adventure as well. Over the years I've had the privilege of talking with many of you in schools, and this book is the result of hearing firsthand what you want to read about most—power-packed action and excitement.

You asked for it—so hang on tight while we jump into another thrilling story in my World of Adventure.

Gary Paulsen

THE
GORGON
SLAYER

CHAPTER 1

Warren Trumbull grunted as he pedaled up the hill. He didn't grunt because the hill was steep —after pedaling up it every weekday since summer vacation had begun, he was used to it. He grunted because he was pedaling for speed. Along the hilltop ran a unicorn crossing.

Warren didn't like anything mythological, and 'corns were the worst. All that stuff the MPS (Mythological Protection Society) put out about them—that they were noble and majestic and held the beauty of the universe in their horns—was garbage. What 'corns did was pop bike tires.

He reached the crossing and sped down the other side of the hill. A shrill whinny and galloping hoofbeats sent a chill up his spine, and he pushed down on the pedal as if he were trying to drive it three feet into the asphalt. Horn hissed on rubber just as he shot away.

"Not today, pinhead!"

Warren laughed at the beautiful white stallion with the golden mane and silver horn as it pranced in frustration behind him. It was the first time in three days that his tire had escaped the 'corn. Today Princey wouldn't threaten to fire him for being late for work. The day was shaping up nicely.

Warren worked for Prince Charming's Damsel in Distress Rescue Agency, doing the assignments that no one else wanted—genuine damsel rescue went to the older guys. Warren was eleven, too young for a real job. He was stuck doing whatever work he could get. Working for Princey wasn't much, but twenty bucks a day out of Princey's grimy pockets was better than nothing.

Some of the guys were already waiting in the bleachers when Warren pedaled up—Rank Frank Divine and his admirers, and a new guy Warren had never seen before. Rank Frank leered at him as he parked beside the garbage can.

"Hey, Piggy, where's the pinhead? You're supposed to show up in fifteen minutes with your tire flapping!"

"Suck on a Hydra, Frank." Warren took a seat three rows up, close to the new guy and well away from Frank and his crowd. They didn't call him Rank Frank for nothing.

"Is Princey here yet?" he asked the new guy, who was wearing a shirt with "Rick" stitched over the pocket.

Rick something-or-other's long head shook slowly on its long neck. "Nope."

"Wouldn't you know it? I'm finally on time, and Princey shows up late."

"That's the breaks, Piggy."

"Don't call me Piggy. My name is Warren."

"I didn't know that."

Warren shrugged his soft, heavy shoulders. "That's all right."

"Okay. My name is Rick Howell. Sorry about the piggy thing."

"Forget it." Warren wished *he* could forget it. The problem was that the nickname fit him so well. He had pink skin and a little piggy nose, turned up at the end so that his nostrils stared everyone he talked to right in the face. His ears stuck out and up—little piggy ears. He looked a little piggy all around.

"Hey, Piggy," Frank called, "why are you here so early? Did someone wake you up by huffing and puffing and blowing your house down?"

Everyone laughed except Warren and Rick. That Divine, he was a real funny guy.

"You know what Neptune's trident is, Frank?" Warren asked.

"That big fork he carries around? I've seen him with it on TV. So?"

"So go sit on it." This time no one laughed but Rick.

It used to be that everyone called Warren Warren. That was before he learned that the old hag who lived next door to him was a witch—a real witch. She caught him late one night raiding her garden. She said that if he was determined to eat like a pig, she'd make it easy for him.

Warren ran around on all fours, squealing, for two whole months. Dr. Fileberg said he was lucky to have recovered as much as he had, but it would go beyond luck for him to recover any further. Warren's father said he hoped Warren had learned his lesson. Warren had.

"Ba-blee-ba-blee-ba-blee, that's all, folks!" Rank Frank whooped.

"Do you know where I live?" Warren asked him.

"Yeah, on Twelfth. Out back in a sty, right?" Frank honked a laugh.

Warren forced a smile. "Good one. Anyway, right next door lives this nice old lady. Growing in her garden are the best watermelons you've ever tasted."

Rank Frank sat forward, suddenly interested. "Really?"

"As soon as the sun goes down, they're yours for the taking."

"All right! Thanks, Piggy!"

"Don't mention it." Warren only hoped that the old hag was into garden slugs now instead of pigs.

The sound of backfire ripped the morning air, and Princey's rusty pickup struggled into the agency's driveway. Princey was a Cyclops, with one eye in the middle of his bald head, scrub brush bristles growing out of his ears, a cigarette dangling from the corner of his mouth, and a constant snarl showing yellow, pointed teeth.

"GRR-OW WITCH!" Princey groaned as he unfolded himself from the pickup's cab. Princey was tall, over eight feet, and pickups were small. Driving to work never left him in a very good mood.

He trudged to the side of the dispatching office—really an old garage—hacked, spit, and unlocked the door. He went inside, and a moment later the garage door opened to reveal Princey leaning on the desk he'd built. He scowled even more than normal and smacked his lips as if he'd eaten a bad skunk for breakfast. His bleary eye scanned the bleachers.

"TRUMBULL! YOU'RE ON TIME!" Princey said everything in capitals.

"Yes, sir," Warren answered.

"WHERE'S O'ROURKE, CHEN, AND HARPER?" Princey waved away any answer. "FORGET IT. I KNOW WHERE THEY ARE." He studied the tattered spiral notebook that served as a work log. "HERE'S TODAY'S ASSIGNMENTS." Princey wasn't much for small talk.

"DIVINE, COME HERE." Rank Frank rose and grinned his way to the desk. He could grin because he knew he was getting the best assignment available. He wasn't named Divine for nothing—his dad was Jupiter, the king of the Olympian gods, and Princey always stayed on Daddy's good side.

"DIVINE, A BEAUTIFUL YOUNG PRINCESS IS TRAPPED IN AN EVIL WARLOCK'S TOWER. TRY TO HAVE HER OUT BEFORE CLOSING, WILL YOU?"

Rank Frank was still grinning. "Sure thing, boss." He wrote down the address from the log and was gone on his fifty-eight-speed touring bike—a gift from his father—before anyone could tell him what a lucky scuzz he was.

"RODRIGUEZ." Rodriguez stepped forward. Princey didn't like Rodriguez, especially when he'd first had to be nice to Frank. "OLD MAN FREDERICK WANTS HIS HORSE BARN CLEANED OUT. FIND A RIVER AND SEE WHAT YOU CAN DO."

Warren groaned in sympathy for Rodriguez. Three thousand years ago, Hercules had cleaned the huge and extremely filthy Augean stables by diverting a river through them. Ever since, Cyclops like Princey always assumed that rivers were the only way to clean stables. Most humans were not as strong as Hercules —actually no humans were; they had to use a shovel. Rodriguez had a manure-filled day ahead of him.

Princey handed out the work assignments, one by one. Thurston had to capture an escaped winged horse; Doolittle had to shingle a witch's candy house with chocolate bars. The bleachers emptied until only Warren and Rick were left.

"TRUMBULL AND . . . YOU, THE NEW GUY."

"Howell," Rick said.

"RIGHT, HOWARD. COME UP HERE."

"Both of us?" Warren asked. He'd never been part of a two-man assignment before.

"BOTH OF YOU. YOU'RE GOING TO TRAIN HOWARD." Princey scanned the work log. "MRS. HELGA THORENSEN CALLED IN THREE DAYS AGO ABOUT A GORGON IN HER BASEMENT. I SENT OUT O'ROURKE, THEN CHEN, AND THEN HARPER, BUT THEY . . ." He waved his hand again. "WELL, YOU KNOW WHAT GORGONS DO."

Warren knew—if you looked at one, you turned to stone. There were animated Gorgons on television commercials, but the censors kept how nasty they looked to a minimum. The commercials always began with a green winged female monster with snakes for hair moving into some poor sucker's attic. Does the sucker want to get rid of her? Of course he does! Run down to your nearest convenience store, sucker, for a jumbo-size can of Gorgon

Gone! And if you act now, you'll also receive a free blindfold!

But the trouble was that Gorgon Gone didn't work. Instead of wasting their money, most people ignored the commercials and called in professional Gorgon exterminators.

"YOU TWO SEE WHAT YOU CAN DO ABOUT IT."

Or two eleven-year-old boys.

Rick didn't look as if he was feeling very well, but he was a rookie and unused to this. Warren didn't feel well because he was more than used to this. He was sick and tired of getting these bottom-of-the-barrel assignments —he'd taken out at least a dozen Gorgons already this summer. They were boring.

The only problem anyone ever had with them was turning into stone, which wasn't much of a problem if you knew what you were doing. If you did harden up, when—or if —someone later exterminated the Gorgon, you'd reflesh with nothing more than a splitting headache, sore muscles, and a gritty taste in your mouth.

If the Gorgon flew off while you were stone, then the problem became much more than just a problem. About all you could hope for then was a nice spot in the park and a nearby sign that read Please Keep the Pigeons Off the Statue. But that never happened. Well, hardly ever, anyway.

Only one thing worried Warren. Three guys had already screwed up. There had to be a reason.

"WHAT ARE YOU WAITING FOR?" Princey demanded. "CHRISTMAS?"

Rick sighed. "Do we have to take this one?"

Princey leaned over the desk. "ROOKIES SHOULDN'T BE SO CHOOSY, HOWARD. RE-MEMBER, YOU'RE ONLY WORKING ON A TRIAL BASIS." He turned his eye on Warren. "WHAT ABOUT YOU, TRUMBULL? DO YOU WANT TO PASS ON THE ASSIGNMENT, OR DO YOU WANT TO KEEP YOUR JOB?"

Warren wasn't sure. He was saving the money he earned for a new camera. The god-dess of love, Venus, was coming to town on the first stop of her latest world tour, and he wanted to get some good pictures. But was a camera worth always getting stuck with the most boring assignments?

Worse yet, what if he and Rick failed? Once they refleshed they'd have to live with the nickname "rockhead" for the rest of their lives. No nickname was as bad as that, except maybe Piggy.

But still, pictures of Venus were worth a few risks.

He looked at Rick. Rick looked at him. They both nodded.

"Could I get that address from you, Princey?" Warren asked.

CHAPTER 2

With Princey's bellow of "COME BACK A ROCKHEAD, AND I'LL DOCK YOU HALF YOUR PAY" ringing in their ears, Rick and Warren set out to do something Rick had never done and Warren didn't want to do. Even so, it would be an easy, if dull, day's work.

"Where do we start?" Rick asked. He didn't have a bike, so he was balancing on Warren's handlebars. He was too tall for Warren to see over, but so thin Warren could almost see through him.

"At Happy Harry's Rent-All," Warren said

patiently. "That's where we get our equipment. Princey has certain procedures we're supposed to follow with Gorgons."

"Procedures?" Rick asked.

"Harry will explain it to you."

Happy Harry's Rent-All rented everything. Everything. If you needed to get somewhere in a hurry and wanted to stay neat doing it, Happy Harry would have a magic carpet with stain guard waiting for you. If a pesky giant was hiding in the clouds above your yard, you could get rid of him with an ax and a magic bean from Happy Harry's. If you needed it, if you wanted it—or even if you didn't—it was waiting on Happy Harry's dusty shelves.

For a price, of course.

"What can I help you good-looking young men with?" Happy Harry asked, his fat cheeks crowding out his Happy Harry smile. "I bet you're helping your dad shingle the roof, and you dropped and lost your hammer. I have just the thing for you."

He pulled a large stone mallet from beneath the counter. "This is Mjollnir, the hammer of the Norse thunder god, Thor. Drop it, and it comes right back to you. I'll let you have it cheap."

I'll just bet that's Thor's hammer, Warren thought. He'd heard of scam artists selling counterfeit heavenly artifacts for a hefty fee. Thor himself had spent four months in jail for peddling fakes. They caught him because he'd forgotten to file Made in Taiwan off the hammer handles. Nobody ever said thunder gods had any brains.

Warren ignored Harry's offer. "We need two Gorgon extermination kits."

"Gorgon problems? Well, it's that time of the year." Harry shook his head in sympathy, though his smile remained the same. "Lucky for you, I just happen to have two of the best kits on the market in storage. I'll be right back."

He waddled into his maze of shelves, humming, banging things together and raising a huge cloud of dust, then waddled back with two shiny shields and two swords.

"This is the Perseus Mark Four Ultra Gorgon extermination system. Let me demonstrate." Harry slipped a shield over one hand

and picked up a sword with the other. "Using the sword is obvious—if you can't figure that part out, you better hire a professional. Just remember to aim for the throat. The only way to kill a Gorgon is to cut the head off."

"I know all this," Warren said, "but you better explain it to him."

Harry turned to Rick. "As far as the shield goes, just read your history book. How did Perseus perform the first extermination?"

"He used his shield as a mirror," Rick said, "to keep from looking at the Gorgon."

"Right. Like this." Harry demonstrated the maneuver. "Always use the shield, boys. If you don't, you'll end up with a high iron count in your blood." He laughed. "Get the joke? Iron, mineral, stone, in your blood, you turn to stone . . . you're not laughing."

"How much?" Warren asked, desperate to change the topic.

"Let's see . . ." Harry stroked the fat hanging beneath his chin. "These things are in high demand nowadays . . . thirty dollars a day should cover it."

"Princey won't let us go any higher than twenty-five. It's a standing rule."

Harry nodded. "You work for Prince Charming? He's a very good customer. For you, twenty-eight fifty."

"But he just told you twenty-five," Rick said.

"And I can't let them go for any less than twenty-eight fifty. I have a son studying at the Midas School of Business. Do you have any idea what they charge?"

"But we can't—"

"But you'll have to," Harry interrupted, "unless you want to try exterminating Gorgons with garbage can lids and Popsicle sticks." He grinned, or widened the grin he already had. "Should I start calling you rockheads now?"

A Centaur—half man, half horse—came into the store. Most Centaurs in town were cabbies. It was the only job they were built to do.

"Well, Ernie!" Harry said, apparently forgetting that Warren and Rick existed. "What can I do for you?"

"I need a new cabby hat, Harry. A customer stole mine."

"How awful!"

Yeah, Warren thought, *how awful.* How awful it would be if Harry didn't give his first customers a little attention. Warren half-considered trying the extermination kit out on Harry. If it was going to cost him three dollars and fifty cents of his own, he might as well get his money's worth.

"Well, you know the nature of the business." Ernie reached back and brushed a fly off his withers. "You take a customer wherever he wants to go for fifty cents, then don't let him off your back for anything less than five dollars. One customer got mad and stole my hat. I need to rent one."

"I have just the thing for you." Harry hurried back along the counter, saw that Rick and Warren were still waiting there, and reached beneath the counter for a magic lamp. He rubbed it and a blue genie appeared.

No big deal, Warren thought, *genies are everywhere.* He once switched his dad's aftershave for a magic lamp. The old man was so surprised he almost dropped the poor genie in the toilet.

"Yes, master?" the genie asked now.

"Take care of these two while I deal with a real customer." Harry shuffled off into his maze of shelves.

The genie looked wearily at Rick and Warren. "How much was Harry going to charge you for these extermination kits?"

Warren's escapade with the witch had taught him never to lie to anything that could throw a spell on him. "Twenty-eight fifty."

"I'll let you have them for fourteen and a quarter."

Warren nodded, a little shocked. "Put them on Prince Charming's account."

With the kits tucked safely under their arms, Rick asked the obvious question. "Why so cheap?"

"That isn't cheap," the genie said, "that's the going rate. Happy Harry is a swindler. There's nothing in this store worth more than fifteen."

"Why do you work for such a cheat?"

The genie sighed. "Do I have a choice? He

found my lamp. But just one more wish and *poof!* I'm out of here."

"Thanks," Rick said.

"Yeah, thanks." As Warren followed Rick out the door, Harry waddled back and tried to settle a tiny hat on the Centaur's head. He said cabby hats were really in demand nowadays, but since Ernie was such a good customer, he would let him have it for only twenty-eight fifty.

"Remind me to talk to Princey about Happy Harry when this is all over," Warren said to Rick.

"You better write it down," Rick said, "just in case being turned to stone affects my memory."

CHAPTER 3

Helga Thorensen lived in a white marble temple with five Greek columns across the front, just like every other house in the city. Rick rang the bell. A woman who had probably been old when the gods were babies answered.

"Ya?" she said in a Scandinavian accent as thick as spoiled cream.

"Helga Thorensen?" Warren asked.

"Ya, that's me."

"Mrs. Thorensen, we're with Prince Charming's Damsel in Distress Rescue Agency. We understand you have a Gorgon in your basement."

Helga blinked her watery eyes. She had long silver hair that instead of staying in the bun on the top of her head was settling down above her eyes, as if she were wearing a sun visor. The last thing she looked like was a damsel.

"Oh, so that Mr. Charming sent out two more of you, hey? I was thinking of how to get rid of the three already in my cellar. Now I have to deal with two more. Jiminey!"

"Not to worry, Mrs. Thorensen." Warren tried to sound as if he did this sort of thing every day, which he pretty much did. "The professionals are here now."

"Ya, you bet. That's what the others said." She waved a meaty hand in their direction as she stepped back into the room. "Come in, and close the door before you let all the flies in. Jiminey!"

The living room looked just as Warren had expected it would—stuffed with things that he guessed Helga considered treasures and everyone else considered junk. On top of the television sat a photo of a farmer trying to keep a team of flying horses from dragging a plow through a second-story window. A plaster cast of Pandora's box rested on the bookshelf near a gilt-edged framed certificate declaring Helga an official voting member of the original Jason and the Argonauts fan club. It reminded Warren of his grandparents' place.

"The cellar is down through the kitchen," Helga said. "If you can't get rid of the Gorgon, I won't pay that Mr. Charming to have his rockheads moved out of here. You tell him that, if you aren't rockheads yourselves."

"Don't worry, Mrs. Thorensen. We'll take care of everything." Warren slipped his shield over his forearm and got a good grip on his sword. He turned to Rick, who was doing the same. "Remember, look only into your shield."

"Right." They headed down the stairs.

Trying to make their feet find the stairs while they looked backward into their shields was tough going. Rick would have fallen if

Warren hadn't been in front of him. Finally their feet found the floor. They scanned the basement.

Dusty pipes hung from the ceiling, and a large door opened onto the backyard. Lawn implements and hand tools lay everywhere. O'Rourke stood by the water heater, one leg raised as if he were running, his sword in the air, and his shield on the floor behind him. Chen and Harper were by the furnace with their swords locked in their stony fists. Chen crouched with his hands to his face. Harper looked fearfully over his shoulder, his expression frozen rock solid.

"None of them were looking at their shields when the Gorgon got them," Rick whispered.

Warren nodded. Only fools looked away from their shields on Gorgon extermination assignments. O'Rourke, Chen, and Harper might have been dummies—they were all good friends of Rank Frank—but they certainly were not fools. Warren didn't like it.

"Speaking of the Gorgon," he said, "where is it?"

An old cedar wardrobe stood in the back by

the lawn mower—the Gorgon could be in it, or behind it. Warren flicked its doors open with the tip of his sword. Nothing. He stabbed behind it, at nothing but air. Rick checked behind the furnace, knocking over Chen and chipping his nose on the floor.

"Nothing," Rick said.

"That's impossible—Gorgons don't just vanish into thin air."

"There's nowhere else for her to hide." Rick paused. "Unless she's behind the—"

His eyes opened wide. A horrid shriek erupted from behind the stairs and clammy, leathery wings exploded into Warren's face. He slammed his eyes shut and beat the Gorgon off, hearing Rick's sword swish through empty air. Warren dove back, rolled on his shoulder, and came up clear, his sword slicing in every direction and his eyes fixed on his shield as he flashed it around the basement.

The Gorgon was perched on Harper's stony arm. She was sixty pounds of boiled-down ugly with a face like a living nightmare. Snakes danced around her head, hissing and

25

striking at Rick's sword as he waved it in the air. Her gold-and-black eyes were slit like a cat's, and her teeth were in worse shape than Princey's.

With one clawed hand, she gathered the dust off the top of a pipe and threw it at Rick's shield.

"Aagh! She messed up my shield! I can't see a thing!"

Panic crawled across Rick's face, the same look that was frozen on Harper's. He dropped his shield and turned toward the Gorgon.

"Don't look, Rick!"

But Rick was thinking—his eyes were closed. He brought his sword around in a long, fast arc, aiming for the Gorgon's neck. But he was swinging blindly. The Gorgon jumped back, hissing, and Rick's sword clanged uselessly off Harper's forehead.

"Harper is going to hate you for that when he refleshes."

"I don't care about Harper! Where am I? Where is the Gorgon? How do I get out of here?"

"I'll get you out!" Warren shouted as he

leaped toward his companion, fighting through foul Gorgon breath as the beast fluttered and shrieked in his face. The Gorgon, beating her wings on Rick's ears like a boxer, was waiting to shout "Surprise!" in whatever language Gorgons shouted as soon as he opened his eyes.

Warren fought closer. The Gorgon retreated to the water heater. Suddenly she leaped up, wiped a pipe clean, and threw a handful of dust at Warren's shield. As he sneezed, a wing smacked the back of his head, his sword flew up, and suddenly dust was everywhere.

When he could see, Warren looked at his shield. If the entire world had turned to dust, then it was still working. Otherwise . . .

"Rick, she got my shield, too!"

"Then close your eyes."

Warren had figured that much out for himself. There was a hissing cackle, and scaly fingers hit him first on one blind side, then on the other. His sword clanged against something hard and vibrated so badly that he dropped it. He wondered if Harper would be mad at him, too, when he refleshed. If he refleshed. If any of them did.

Warren reached for the sword, but the wings beat him silly. He kicked something and heard the sword skitter away.

"I've lost my sword, Rick. Where are you?"

"Over here."

"Over here" could be just about anywhere. As Warren stumbled toward Rick's voice, his useless shield banged hollowly against a metal cylinder.

Okay, he thought, *that was the water heater. If it's here, then a step in this direction will put the staircase straight ahead, and if Rick hasn't moved, then another step this way and . . .*

The whistle of a blade swished by a quarter of an inch from his nose.

"Stop swinging your sword, Rick! You'll behead me instead of the Gorgon."

"Sorry. Snaky-brain gives me the willies. Where are you, anyway?"

"I'm right here, about . . . Aah!" Clawed fingers dug into Warren's face, and he fell. Clawed fingers must have dug into Rick's

face, too, because he aahed and fell on Warren.

"Get off me, Rick." He was about to open
his eyes, to take a chance at turning to stone
in order to find their way out, when a hand
clamped over his face.

"No you don't," Rick scolded. "No peeking.
If you turn into a rockhead, then I have to kill
the thing myself."

"How did you know I was opening my
eyes?"

"I was watching."

Warren slapped his hand over Rick's face.
"Then no *you* don't!"

They lay on the floor, clutching each other's
heads, with the Gorgon flapping and screaming above them.

"Is this really worth a new camera?" Warren asked.

"Is this really worth a new bike?" Rick
wondered aloud.

The Gorgon swooped, slapped them with
her wings, then was gone. Just as Warren began to believe that she was *really* gone, she
swooped and slapped them again.

"Where are the stairs?" Rick tried to shake his head free, but Warren held tight.

"As near as I can figure, about six feet in the direction of your right shoulder."

"Then on the count of three we stand and make a run for it. One . . . two . . . three!"

The stairs were only five feet away, and running six feet left Warren and Rick sprawled across them with bruises on their shins and bumps on their noses.

They struggled up the rest of the way, banging arms, bashing ribs, and jamming elbows into each other's mouths. The Gorgon backed off just as they reached the top. The two boys scrambled breathlessly into the kitchen.

"That Gorgon is one tough cookie," Rick said.

Warren rolled on his back, panting. "All I know is that it could really use a good hair conditioner."

CHAPTER 4

"Thor's bolts!"

Above them, as threatening as an avalanche, towered a scowling Helga Thorensen. From Warren's flat-on-his-back viewpoint, her hands on her hips looked three miles apart.

"So that's the best you can do? You can't take care of a simple thing like a Gorgon?"

"That's no ordinary Gorgon, Mrs. Thorensen," Warren said. "That Gorgon could be in a horror movie."

Helga grunted. "That's a good one. I suppose that next you'll say that dandelions should be in horror movies, too, or baby chicks." She shook her head.

Warren rolled onto his stomach. "I know it sounds crazy, Mrs. Thorensen, but this isn't a Gorgon I want to mess with again."

"Me either." Rick nodded. "If I were you, I'd just let her have the basement. There's nothing down there but a couple of rock-heads, anyway."

"Ya, sure. Where do you think I keep my lawn equipment, hey? What I've got here is a couple of wimps."

She stopped shaking her head, rested a minute, and shook it harder. "In my day we didn't have fancy store-bought swords and shields for Gorgon killing. We had to make our own. If we wanted to kill a Gorgon, we had to find her ourselves. Many was the day that I walked seven miles through four feet of snow, barefoot, to find a Gorgon, and the roads to her and back were both uphill."

"Please, Mrs. Thorensen . . ."

"And you didn't hear me bellyaching because the nasty old Gorgon was a little meaner than usual. If you can't get a simple job like this done, then I'll have to call your boss and tell him so."

"Please, Mrs. Thorensen," Warren pleaded, "he'll fire me. I've been late for the last three mornings. One more screwup and I'm gone."

"And I'm still on a trial basis," Rick said. "I'm gone, too."

"If you can't do the job, then you shouldn't be working at it." Helga picked up the phone. As she began to dial Princey's number, Warren scrambled to his feet and slammed his hand down on the cradle.

"All right, Mrs. Thorensen," he said, "you win. We'll go back down there and get the Gorgon."

CHAPTER 5

The trouble with the Gorgon was this: Gorgons weren't supposed to throw dust on shields —they weren't supposed to be smart enough to know what the shields were for. How many brains can you have with snakes growing out of your head?

"I suppose it's evolution," Warren said. He was leaning against the basement door like a prisoner awaiting execution. He had Helga, who was now puttering around in her garden, to thank for that. "After three thousand years, one of them has finally figured out the Perseus method of Gorgon extermination."

"But why did the one have to be ours?" Rick asked. "Why couldn't evolution have waited until after I got my new bike?"

Warren shook his head. "Asking questions like that won't do us any good. We need to figure out how to make the best use of our assets, plan our attack, and then get down there and cut old Snaky-brain's noggin off. Let's begin with our assets. We have two brains, both of which are better than the Gorgon's—"

"Or should be," Rick said.

"Okay, we have two brains that *should* be better than the Gorgon's. We only have one sword—I dropped mine in the basement."

"And we only have one shield. Mine is lying next to Harper." Rick leaned back against the refrigerator. "A shield won't help, anyway. You saw what the Gorgon did to them."

"Yeah, you're right." Warren rubbed his chin. "But maybe you aren't. Did you notice how the Gorgon always flew to where she would be in line with the shield, so she could throw dust on it?"

"I didn't have time to notice anything."

"Well, she did. If the Gorgon follows shields, we can use the one we have to control where she flies."

"What do you mean?"

"Let's say we want her by the water heater. If I hold the shield so the water heater is reflected in it, then that's where the Gorgon will go."

"So what you're saying is that you can position the Gorgon to where I'll be standing with the sword."

"You got it."

"I don't have anything. How am I supposed to aim my swing when I don't dare look to aim it?"

"I'll tell you where to swing."

"You can't tell a rockhead anything, and that's what I'll be. You know how hard it is to keep your eyes closed down there? If you don't, ask Chen, O'Rourke, or Harper."

"We'll think of something."

The back door opened and Helga stuck her head into the kitchen. "When are you two going to get to work, hey? I have a yard to trim.

My electric weed trimmer is in the basement."

"We're just about set to go, Mrs. Thorensen."

"Ya, ya, sure you are. Lollygagging around
is what you're doing. Don't expect much of a
tip." She thumped back outside.

Rick shook his head doubtfully. "I don't
know about this plan. It sounds pretty risky."

"You want that new bike, don't you?"

Five minutes later, Warren was peering into
the remaining shield and leading Rick down
the basement stairs. Rick was carrying the
sword and wearing a grocery bag over his
head that they'd borrowed from Helga. The
dust still in the air tickled Warren's nose,
making him sneeze.

"Is that the Gorgon?" Rick swung the
sword. Warren had to duck to avoid a perma-
nent crew cut.

"Will you be careful with that thing?"

"Sorry. I'm a little nervous."

"Don't swing until I tell you to."

Warren flashed the shield beneath the stairs.

No Gorgon. He flashed it at the water heater, and at all the rockheads. No Gorgons there, either. He checked behind the furnace, Rick stumbling along blindly behind him. The Gorgon seemed to have disappeared.

"I don't understand it," Warren said. "I don't know where she is."

"Don't ask me to help you find her."

Something was wrong with the wardrobe—the door was barely cracked open. Warren had opened it wide the last time they were in the basement.

"I think I know where she is," he whispered.

"Do you want me to swing now?" Rick whispered back.

"I'll tell you when."

A flicker of tongue licked by the edge of the open door—a flicker of a snake's tongue. "She's in the wardrobe."

"What'll we do?"

"When I say 'leap,' leap straight ahead about three feet. I'll open the door and use the shield to position the Gorgon right in front of you. When everything is right, I'll yell 'swing,' and two seconds after I do, I want to see twenty snakes and one very ugly head rolling across the floor."

"No problem," Rick said. "You can count on me."

Warren crouched, his legs as tight as steel springs. "Leap!"

Warren bounded ahead, with Rick right behind him. The Gorgon exploded from behind the door like a grenade. Warren whipped the shield around until Rick was reflected in it. The Gorgon followed the shield's movement until her scaly green neck was only a foot away from the sword's gleaming blade, which was held like a baseball bat over Rick's shoulder.

"Now, Rick. Swing!"

Rick just stood there. The Gorgon shrieked and hissed only inches from his face, and he just stood there.

"Swing, Rick, swing!"

Rick stared at him stonily. Warren froze as if he'd suddenly been shoved into a freezer. Rick, he realized, shouldn't be staring at him at all.

Warren turned the shield to look at the floor. The grocery bag was lying there. It should have been on Rick's head. One of the ceiling pipes must have knocked it off when Rick leaped toward the wardrobe.

"Oh, no. Not you, too, Rick."

Rick didn't answer. He had turned into a rockhead.

Chapter 6

I wonder, Warren thought as he dropped to the floor, lost his shield, and covered his eyes, *if it would be possible to have a worse day.*

The Gorgon's feet pounded up and down Warren's spine, her fingers tried to tear his hands away from his eyes, and her mouth poured screams into his ear. Snakes slithered across his eyebrows.

"Get off me!" He rolled over. The Gorgon lifted into the air, and a blind but very lucky kick sent her careening off what could have been the furnace. Warren scrambled to his feet and took off in what he thought was the direction of the staircase. He ended up in the wardrobe.

The door closed behind him and he gained a second of peace. Outside, the sound of the Gorgon's wings got louder, then softer, then louder again before their beating stopped altogether.

She's waiting for me, Warren thought. *Out there, somewhere. I'll peek out and see her grinning, nasty face, and I'll be a stone Warren in a wardrobe, like an overgrown knick-knack on a shelf.*

"I wish things were like the good old days," he said aloud, fear raising his voice an octave too high, "when all I had to worry about was being a pig."

What I need, he thought after he'd swallowed his panic down far enough so that he could think, *is a sword.* Of course, having a sword hadn't done him much good so far. *What I need,* he rethought, *is a hundred guys with a hundred swords.* But he only had four guys, and they were all rockheads, and their swords were trapped in their stony grips.

My sword is still out there, he remembered. *Somewhere.*

He had to find that sword. It was hidden in a dark basement filled with lawn tools. He had to find it with his eyes closed. A dragon lady with enough ugly on her to pave a parking lot would be screaming and clawing at his face.

Impossible.

I could flee up the stairs instead, he thought, *then get fired by Princey and have to live with the knowledge that I wasn't able to do a simple thing like exterminate a Gorgon. I'd rather be a park statue.*

Faced with a choice between the impossible and the unwanted, Warren chose the impossible. So what if there was no way he could ever find the sword? He would just have to.

And he would just have to do it now.

He burst out of the wardrobe, his hands covering his eyes, shouting a battle cry he had heard in an old war movie. He tripped over something—probably Rick's granite foot—scrambled back up, and ran into the wall. He fell into a pile of tools.

The Gorgon was all over him, as usual. Warren kept his eyes covered with one hand and searched frantically through the tools with the other.

He found a hammer. No good, it didn't cut. He found a pair of pliers. It didn't cut either, and pinching her head off would take too long and be too messy. Where was that sword?

He stood and the Gorgon pushed him back down. He landed on Helga's electric weed trimmer.

Weed trimmer, Warren thought, *hmmm.*

He felt down the trimmer's shaft to its business end, the Gorgon gnawing at his fingers as he did. He found the motor, then the safety guard. He felt beneath it to see if the shaft was loaded with trimming line. It was. He worked his hand back to the other end, found the trigger, and pressed it. Nothing happened.

You have to plug it in, you dummy, his mind shouted over the Gorgon's screams.

He found the plug, then felt along the wall. Miracle of miracles, there was an outlet right next to his shoulder. He couldn't get the plug in. Without thinking, he opened his eyes to see why.

He had the plug sideways, with the tongs on the top and the bottom. He straightened it out and fitted it into the outlet. As he did, a snake dropped down and hissed in his eyes. Warren was face-to-face with the Gorgon.

His nose suddenly went numb. When he touched it with his finger, he heard a clink.

Hurry, his mind shouted at him, *before it's too late!*

When Warren pressed the trigger, he couldn't feel it. The only way he knew the trimmer was working was the zinging sound the trimming line made as the motor twirled it in the air.

"Not yet, Snaky-brain!"

He rolled on his back, his eyes clenched shut again, and kicked his suddenly very heavy legs straight into the air. They hit something solid. He swept the weed trimmer in an arc over his head as if he were taking out the biggest thistle in the world.

Zing!

Something splattered wetly beside him. Something else thumped to the floor at his feet. He thought he knew what they were, but he didn't want to risk looking. He didn't open his eyes until he heard Chen groan something about his nose and heard Harper say, "Oh man, who belted me in the forehead?"

CHAPTER 7

Princey scowled even more than usual. His eye searched the five embarrassed faces of O'Rourke, Chen, Harper, Rick, and Warren. They had good reason to be embarrassed. Princey didn't like bungled assignments.

"WHO SHOULD I BLAME?" he roared.

"Blame them all, boss," Rank Frank said from the bleachers. "Especially Piggy."

"Go kiss a troll, Frank," Warren said.

Rank Frank laughed. "Nothing you say can ruin my mood, Piggy. I have a date with a princess tonight."

"Are you going to take her watermelon hunting?"

Frank grinned. "I'm thinking about it."

"CAN WE GET BACK TO THE MATTER AT HAND?" Princey bellowed. "WHO SHOULD I BLAME?"

No one answered.

"WELL?"

Still no one answered. Princey shook his head and cleaned out his ear with one huge pinky, after forcing the bristles aside. "THEN I GUESS I'LL BLAME YOU ALL. HALF PAY FOR ROCKHEADS." His big mitt slapped a wadded ten-dollar bill into each of the first four employees' hands, then slapped one into Warren's.

"But I'm not a rockhead," Warren said meekly. "Not really."

"YOU GET HALF PAY FOR VIOLATING PROCEDURES."

"Huh?"

"YOU'RE SUPPOSED TO KILL GORGONS WITH SWORDS, NOT WITH WEED TRIMMERS."

Warren sighed and took his pay. It was best not to argue with Princey.

Princey paid everyone else his twenty dollars. Poor Rodriguez would have to spend half of his on a manure fumigating service.

"I'll see you tomorrow, Princey," Warren said.

"RIGHT, TOMORROW. LET'S SEE IF YOU CAN MAKE IT ON TIME TWO DAYS IN A ROW, OKAY?"

Warren was going to tell Princey about how Happy Harry was ripping him off, but decided not to.

Princey hacked, spit, and lit a cigarette. Still scowling, he closed the garage door, then crammed himself into his pickup and thundered away.

Warren joined Rick in staring glumly at their pay. "Not much for all we went through today, is it?" Rick asked.

"Not much," Warren agreed. "Ten bucks and no tip."

"Are you going to be here tomorrow, or were you just telling Princey a story?"

"I'll be here tomorrow."

Rick sighed. "I guess I will be, too. I really need that new bike. I'll see you."

"Yeah," Warren said, "I'll see you." He watched as Rick walked stiffly away, then climbed, groaning, onto his bicycle. His legs screamed from the pain of the minor refleshing they'd undergone.

"Hopefully," he said to himself, "they aren't so sore that they can't speed me past the unicorn crossing."

"Beware of the sausage maker on your ride home, Piggy." Rank Frank laughed.

"Go kiss Medusa, Frank." Warren pedaled painfully away.

The sun was setting. The air was summer-evening cool, with birds singing sweetly in the trees. A fairy family was having a picnic on a napkin across the street—a corn kernel, a whole thimbleful of soda, and a miniature marshmallow for dessert. It promised to be a beautiful evening.

Warren sighed. If only tomorrow would hold so much promise.

Tomorrow was just another day working at

Prince Charming's Damsel in Distress Rescue Agency. If Warren was unlucky, and after today he had no reason to think he wouldn't be, it would be another day of lousy assignments at half pay.

But maybe things will be different, he thought. *Maybe I'll get lucky. Maybe I'll get an easy assignment—like slaying a dragon.*

GARY PAULSEN
ADVENTURE GUIDE

HEROES OF MYTHOLOGY

The ancient Greeks believed that the world was flat and circular and that the only existing sea, the Mediterranean, was filled with dragons, monsters, and enchantresses. Believing in heroes and gods who championed the common man gave people a sense of well-being and security.

HERCULES—the son of the god Zeus and a mortal woman, Alcmene. This hero was famous for his strength and courage. His most outstanding exploits were his twelve labors. The sixth of those labors, which is mentioned in this book, was cleaning the stables of King Augeas by running rivers through them.

JASON—the son of King Aeson of Thessaly. Jason was raised by the centaur Chiron. When he was grown up and ready to take his place on the throne of Thessaly, he found that it had been usurped by his uncle Pelias. Pelias promised to give the throne back if Jason could bring him the Golden Fleece from Colchis. Jason led a band of heroes, called the Argonauts, on a successful mission to find the pure gold wool of the sacred ram.

ORPHEUS—the son of the muse Calliope. Orpheus went to the god of the underworld, Pluto, to rescue his wife from him. Orpheus' singing was so beautiful and sad that Pluto let him take her. There was one condition: He couldn't look back at her as they left the underworld. Out of concern, Orpheus glanced back, and his wife was lost to him forever.

THESEUS—the son of Aegeus of Athens. This hero was one of Jason's band of Argonauts and was involved in several fantastic adventures. He was most famous for killing the Minotaur, a monster with the head of a bull and the body of a man.

PERSEUS—the son of Zeus and Danäe. With the help of a helmet of invisibility, Athena's shield, and Hermes' sword, he cut off the head of the Gorgon Medusa. He looked into the shield to escape her gaze, which would have turned him to stone.

ACHILLES—the son of a nymph and Peleus. He was a great hero of the Trojan war. When he was a baby, he was dipped into the river Styx to make him invincible. His mother held him by the heel, which became the only spot on Achilles' body that could be hurt. During the Trojan war he was shot in the heel with an arrow, and he died near the main gate of Troy.

Don't miss all the exciting action!

Rodomonte, an evil giant waiting to do battle within his hidden castle.

But soon after they play the game, strange things start happening to Brett and Tom. The computer is taking over their minds. Now everything that happens in the game is happening in real life. A buzz-bug could gnaw off their ears. Rodomonte could smash them to bits. Brett and Tom have no choice but to play Rodomonte's Revenge again. This time they'll be playing for their lives.

Escape from Fire Mountain

". . . please, anybody . . . fire . . . need help."

That's the urgent cry thirteen-year-old Nikki Roberts hears over the CB radio the weekend she's left alone in her family's hunting lodge. The message also says that the sender is trapped near a bend in the river. Nikki knows it's dangerous, but she has to try to help. She paddles her canoe downriver, coming closer to the thick black smoke of the forest fire with each stroke. When she reaches the bend, Nikki climbs onshore. There, covered with soot and huddled on a rock ledge, sit two small children.

Nikki struggles to get the children to safety. Flames roar around them. Trees splinter to the ground. But as Nikki tries to escape the fire, she doesn't know that two poachers are also hot on her trail. They fear that she and the children have seen too much of their illegal operation—and they'll do anything to keep the kids from making it back to the lodge alive.

The Rock Jockeys

Devil's Wall.

Rick Williams and his friends J.D. and Spud—the Rock Jockeys—are attempting to become the first and youngest climbers to ascend the north face of their area's most treacherous mountain. They're also out to discover if a B-17 bomber rumored to have crashed into the mountain years ago is really there.

As the Rock Jockeys explore Devil's Wall, they stumble upon the plane's battered shell. Inside, they find items that seem to have belonged to the crew, including a diary written by the navigator. Spud later falls into a deep hole and finds something even more frightening: a human skull and bones. To find out where they might have come from, the boys read the navigator's story in the diary. It reveals a gruesome secret that heightens the dangers the mountain might hold for the Rock Jockeys.

Hook 'Em, Snotty!

Bobbie Walker loves working on her grandfather's ranch. She hates the fact that her cousin Alex is coming up from Los Angeles to visit and will probably ruin her summer. Alex can barely ride a horse and doesn't know the first thing about roping. There is no way Alex can survive a ride into the flats to round up wild cattle. But Bobbie is going to have to let her tag along anyway.

Out in the flats the weather turns bad. Even worse, Bobbie knows that she'll have to watch out for the

Bledsoe boys, two mischievous brothers who are usually up to no good. When the boys rustle the girls' cattle, Bobbie and Alex team up to teach the Bledsoes a lesson. But with the wild bull Diablo on the loose, the fun and games may soon turn deadly serious.

Danger on Midnight River

Daniel Martin doesn't want to go to Camp Eagle Nest. He wants to spend the summer as he always does: with his uncle Smitty in the Rocky Mountains. Daniel is a slow learner, but most other kids call him retarded. Daniel knows that at camp, things are only going to get worse. His nightmare comes true when he and three bullies must ride the camp van together.

On the trip to camp Daniel is the butt of the bullies' jokes. He ignores them and concentrates on the roads outside. He thinks they may be lost. As the van crosses a wooden bridge, the planks suddenly give way. The van plunges into the raging river below. Daniel struggles to shore, but the driver and the other boys are nowhere to be found. It's freezing, and night is setting in. Daniel faces a difficult decision. He could save himself . . . or risk everything to try to rescue the others, too.

Look for these thrill-packed adventures coming soon!

Captive!

Roman Sanchez is trying hard to deal with the death of his dad—a SWAT team member gunned down in the line of duty. But Roman's nightmare is just beginning.

When masked gunmen storm into his classroom, Roman and three other boys are taken hostage. They are thrown into the back of a truck and hauled to a run-down mountain cabin, miles from anywhere. They are bound with rope and given no food. With each passing hour the kidnappers deadly threats become even more real.

Roman knows time is running out. Now he must somehow put his dad's death behind him so that he and the others can launch a last desperate fight for freedom.

Project: A Perfect World

When Jim Stanton's family moves to a small town in New Mexico, everyone but Jim is happy. His dad has a great job as a research scientist at Folsum Laboratories. His mom has a beautiful new house. Folsum Labs even buys a bunch of new toys for his little sister.

But there's something strange about the town. The people all dress and act alike. Everyone's *too* polite.

And they're all eerily obedient to the bosses at Folsum Labs.

Though he has been warned not to leave town, Jim wanders into the nearby mountains looking for excitement. There he meets Maria, a mountain girl with a shocking secret that involves Folsum Laboratories, a dangerous mind control experiment, and— most frightening of all—Jim's family.

**Cool sleuths, hot on the case!
Read Gary Paulsen's hilarious
Culpepper Adventures.**

Dunc and Amos Meet the Slasher

Why is mild-mannered Amos dressing in leather, slicking back his hair, strutting around the cafeteria, and going by a phony name? Could it be because of that new kid, Slasher, who's promised to eat Amos for lunch? Or has Amos secretly gone undercover? Amos and his pal Dunc have some hot leads and are close to cracking a stolen stereo racket, but Dunc is worried Amos has taken things too far!

Dunc and the Greased Sticks of Doom

Five . . . four . . . three . . . two . . . Olympic superstar Francesco Bartoli is about to hurl himself down the face of a mountain in another attempt to clinch the world slalom speed record. Cheering fans and snapping cameras are everywhere. But someone is out to stop him, and Dunc thinks he knows who it is. Can Dunc get to the gate in time to save the day? Will Amos survive longer than fifteen minutes on the icy slopes?

Amos's Killer Concert Caper

Amos is desperate. He's desperate for two tickets to the romantic event of his young life . . . the Road Kill concert! He'll do anything to get them because he heard from a friend of a friend of a friend of Melissa Hansen that she's way into Road Kill. But when he enlists the help of his best friend, Dunc, he winds up with more than he bargained for . . . backstage, with a mystery to solve.

Amos Gets Married

Everybody knows Amos Binder is crazy in love with Melissa Hansen. Only, Melissa hasn't given any indication that she even knows Amos exists as a life-form. That is, until now. Suddenly, things with Melissa are different. A wave, a wink—an affectionate "snookems"?! Can this really be Melissa . . . and *Amos*? Dunc is determined to get to the bottom of it all, but who can blame Amos if his feet don't touch the ground?

For laugh-out-loud fun, join Dunc and Amos and take the Culpepper challenge!
Gary Paulsen's Culpepper Adventures—
Bet you can't read just one!

☐ 0-440-40790-7 DUNC AND AMOS AND THE RED TATTOOS.....$3.25/$3.99 Can.

☐ 0-440-40874-1 DUNC'S UNDERCOVER CHRISTMAS................$3.50/$4.50 Can.

☐ 0-440-40883-0 THE WILD CULPEPPER CRUISE......................$3.50/$4.50 Can.

☐ 0-440-40893-8 DUNC AND THE HAUNTED CASTLE.................$3.50/$4.50 Can.

☐ 0-440-40902-0 COWPOKES AND DESPERADOES...................$3.50/$4.50 Can.

☐ 0-440-40920-4 PRINCE AMOS.......................................$3.50/$4.50 Can.

☐ 0-440-40930-6 COACH AMOS..$3.50/$4.50 Can.

☐ 0-440-40990-X AMOS AND THE ALIENS................................$3.50/$4.50 Can.

Bantam Doubleday Dell Books for Young Readers
2451 South Wolf Road
Des Plaines, IL 60018

Please send the items I have checked above. I'm enclosing $_____ (please add $2.50 to cover postage and handling). Send check or money order, no cash or C.O.D.s please.

Name _____

Address _____

City _____ State _____ Zip _____

Please allow four to six weeks for delivery.
Prices and availability subject to change without notice.   BFYR 29 6/94

CHART YOUR COURSE TO EXCITEMENT!

Take the journey of a lifetime with *Gary Paulsen World of Adventure!* Every story is a thrilling, action-packed odyssey, containing an adventure guide with important survival tips no camper or adventurer should be without!

Order any or all of these exciting **Gary Paulsen** adventures. Just check off the titles you want, then fill out and mail the order form below.

☐	0-440-41023-1	**LEGEND OF RED HORSE CAVERN**	$3.50/$4.50 Can.
☐	0-440-41024-X	**RODOMONTE'S REVENGE**	$3.50/$4.50 Can.
☐	0-440-41025-8	**ESCAPE FROM FIRE MOUNTAIN**	$3.50/$4.50 Can.
☐	0-440-41026-6	**THE ROCK JOCKEYS**	$3.50/$4.50 Can.

Bantam Doubleday Dell
Books For Young Readers

BDD BOOKS FOR YOUNG READERS
2451 South Wolf Road
Des Plaines, IL 60018

Please send me the items I have checked above. I am enclosing $_____
(please add $2.50 to cover postage and handling).
Send check or money order, no cash or C.O.D.s please.

NAME _____

ADDRESS _____

CITY _____ STATE _____ ZIP _____

Please allow four to six weeks for delivery.
Prices and availability subject to change without notice.   BFYR 115 3/95